D1489339

DATE DUE

The Lovable Ladybug

Becky Freeman

Illustrated by
Matt Archambault

A Faith Parenting Guide can be found on page 32.

Faith Kids™ is an imprint of
Cook Communications Ministries, Colorado Springs, Colorado 80918
Cook Communications, Paris, Ontario
Kingsway Communications, Eastbourne, England

THE LOVABLE LADYBUG
© 2000 by Becky Freeman for text and Matt Archaumbault for illustrations.

Faith Kids™ is a registered trademark of Cook Communications Ministries.

Published in association with the literary agency of Alive Communications, Inc., 1465 Kelly
Johnson Blvd., Suite 320, Colorado Springs, CO 80920.

Edited by Jeannie Harmon
Designed by Ya Ye Design

Scripture taken from the *Holy Bible: New International Version®* copyright © 1973, 1978, 1984 by
International Bible Society. Used by permission of Zondervan Publishing House. All rights
reserved.

First printing, 2000
Printed in Singapore
04 03 02 01 00   5 4 3 2 1

Library of Congress Cataloging-in-Publication Data

Freeman, Becky, 1959-
    The lovable ladybug / Becky Freeman; illustrated by Matt Archambault.
        p. cm. -- (Gabe & critters)
    Summary: Gabe's new friend Dottie loves polka dots so he gives her a ladybug
as a gift. Includes factual information about ladybugs.
    ISBN 0-7814-3341-X
    [1. Ladybugs--Fiction. 2. Christian life --Fiction.] I. Archambault,
Matthew, ill. II. Title.
PZ7.F874635 Lo2000
[Fic]--dc21

                                                                              99-053239
                                                                              CIP

Dedicated to:
My youngest son, Gabe,
a true critter-lover and
the inspiration for this series.
Thanks for the "worm" memories
. . . and for the hugs.
Love,
Mom

The bell rang and Gabe ran out the door. Recess was his favorite part of the school day. But while the other kids climbed monkey bars and played kickball, Gabe and his friend, Josh, went looking for critters.

Gabe was playing with a fuzzy caterpillar when a little girl with boing-yoing curls and a purple polka-dotted dress walked up.

"Why is that worm wearing a sweater?" she asked.

Gabe laughed and began to tell her all about caterpillars—how they spin cocoons. He stopped in the middle of explaining how caterpillars turn into butterflies and asked, "What's your name?"

5

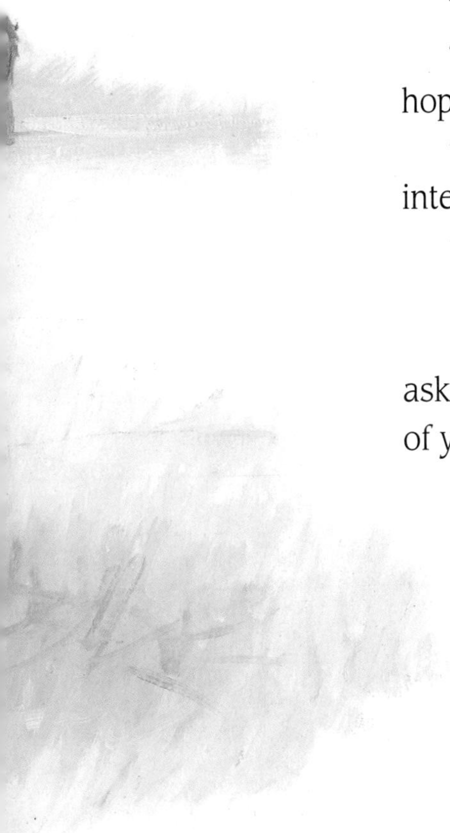

"Dottie," she replied cheerfully. "Is that why you wear dots?"

"Yes, I LOVE polka-dots."

"Oh," said Gabe. "Hey, how come you aren't playing hopscotch with those girls over there?"

"I don't like hopscotch," said Dottie. "I'd rather look for interesting things. Flowers, rocks, . . ."

"Critters?" asked Gabe.

"Yes, I LOVE critters!"

Gabe paused a moment, until he felt brave enough to ask Dottie one more question. "Dottie, could I pull on one of your curls?"

"I guess so," she giggled, "but don't pull too hard!"

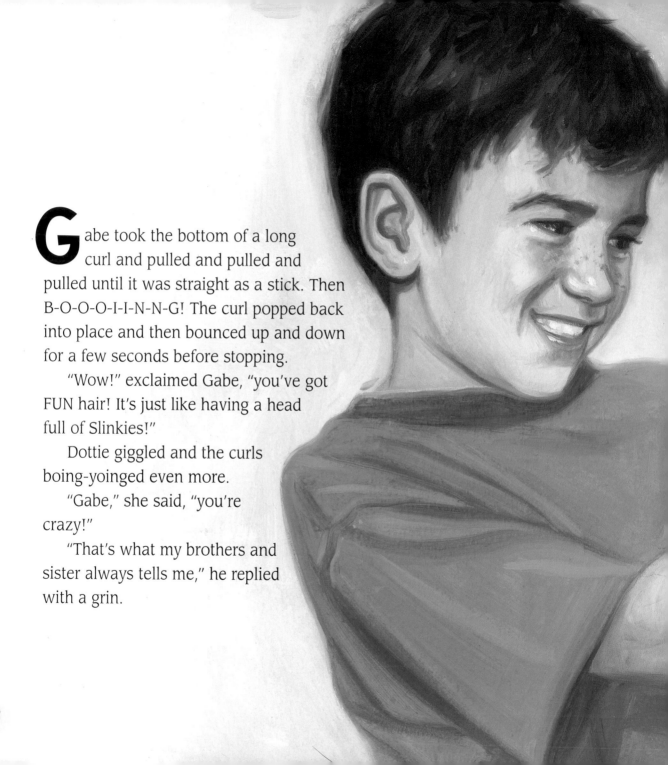

G abe took the bottom of a long curl and pulled and pulled and pulled until it was straight as a stick. Then B-O-O-O-I-I-N-N-G! The curl popped back into place and then bounced up and down for a few seconds before stopping.

"Wow!" exclaimed Gabe, "you've got FUN hair! It's just like having a head full of Slinkies!"

Dottie giggled and the curls boing-yoinged even more.

"Gabe," she said, "you're crazy!"

"That's what my brothers and sister always tells me," he replied with a grin.

About that time Josh hollered across the field. "Hey, Gabe! Come see how many grasshoppers you can catch with one hand!"

Gabe ran over and snatched up a handful of grasshoppers. There were so many insects hopping that the grass sounded as though it were buzzing.

"Who were you talking to?" asked Josh.

"The new girl," answered Gabe. "Her name is Dottie. She likes polka-dots . . . and worms that wear sweaters."

"Huh?" Josh asked, as he scratched his head, but Gabe couldn't explain because the bell rang and everyone had to go back to class.

After school, Gabe ran into the house and fixed himself a whole peanut butter, pickle, and potato chip sandwich with raspberry jelly on top. He finished it off with a glass of cold milk. Then he walked down the hall to his big sister's room and knocked on the door.

"Who is it?" she asked.

"It's me, Gabe! I need to ask you something."

Rachel opened the door, pulling off her earphones so she could hear Gabe's voice.

"Rachel," he said, "I need to know what kind of stuff girls like."

"Why?" she asked suspiciously.

"I met a new friend today," Gabe said, "and I just wanted to give her something."

"Well," said Rachel as she plopped down on her bed, resting her head on her hands. "Nearly all girls like jewelry—you know, necklaces and earrings and stuff."

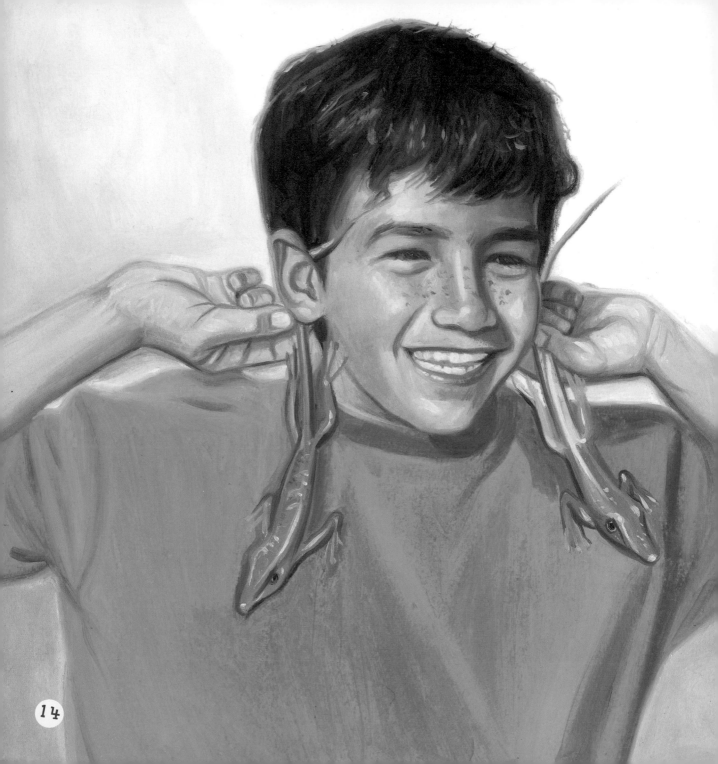

14

Gabe smiled.

   He turned and ran outside and within a few minutes, Rachel heard another knock at her door. When she opened it, there stood Gabe with a green anole dangling from each ear.

   "Do you think a girl would like these? They even change colors!"

   "Gabe," said Rachel as she shook her head, "you are CRAZY."

   "In a good way or a bad way?" he asked.

   "Well, sometimes in a good way and sometimes in a not-so-good way. But I think you should find something else for your new friend. Girls don't like earrings that wiggle and bite."

Gabe sighed. He went back outside and let the anoles go. Then he started looking again for something special to bring to school. He came upon a beautiful garden snake sunning itself on a rock. Gabe gently picked it up and wrapped it around himself like a necklace. Then he remembered that Josh told him all girls are afraid of snakes. Nothing seemed right.

Just before suppertime as Gabe was picking string beans from the garden, he spotted something on a tomato plant's leaf. It was the perfect answer to his search. He could hardly wait until tomorrow.

That night Gabe found a small empty box, spread glue all over it, then covered it with all the bubble gum wrappers he'd been saving in his treasure box. When it was dry, he poked holes in the top with a pencil and put a little leftover worm dirt in the bottom.

During recess the next day at school, Gabe found Dottie and handed her the box.

"What's this?" Dottie asked.

"It's for you. I just thought you might like it."

"Thank you," said Dottie.

Gabe couldn't help but notice how shiny her curls looked in the sunlight, dangling beneath her pink polka-dotted bow. He so wanted to stretch out one of those curls as hard as he could and watch it boing-yoing back, but he knew he'd better not. He didn't want to wear out her hair.

Dottie opened the box and let out a squeal.

"Uh-oh," said Gabe, "are you afraid of bugs?"

"No, you Silly," Dottie said as she grinned, "sometimes I squeal when I'm happy. I LOVE ladybugs. God made them so small and smooth and colorful and, and . . ."

"Polka-dotted," added Gabe. "Yes! Polka-dotted. Gabe, you're a nice friend. Thank you."

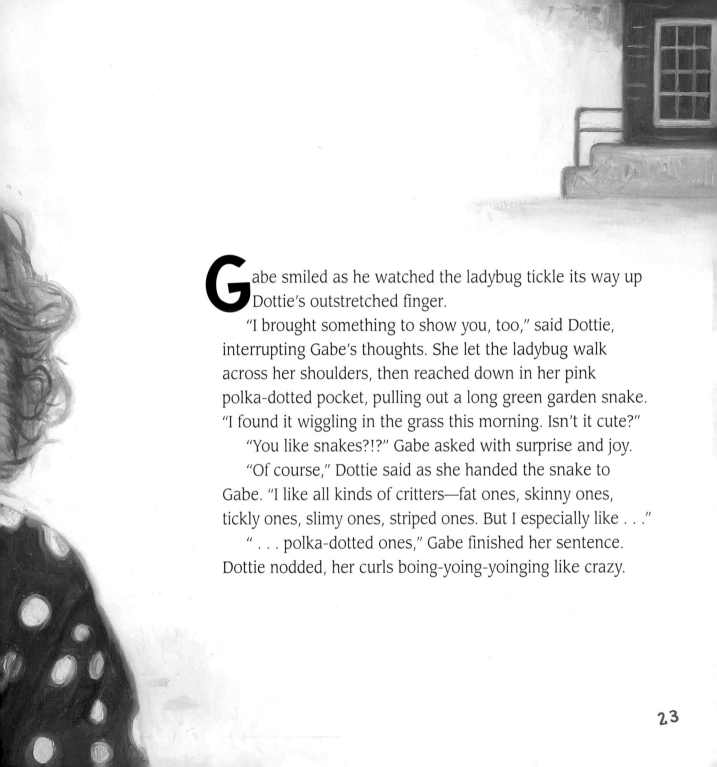

Gabe smiled as he watched the ladybug tickle its way up Dottie's outstretched finger.

"I brought something to show you, too," said Dottie, interrupting Gabe's thoughts. She let the ladybug walk across her shoulders, then reached down in her pink polka-dotted pocket, pulling out a long green garden snake. "I found it wiggling in the grass this morning. Isn't it cute?"

"You like snakes?!?" Gabe asked with surprise and joy.

"Of course," Dottie said as she handed the snake to Gabe. "I like all kinds of critters—fat ones, skinny ones, tickly ones, slimy ones, striped ones. But I especially like . . ."

" . . . polka-dotted ones," Gabe finished her sentence. Dottie nodded, her curls boing-yoing-yoinging like crazy.

23

Later that night as Gabe sat in his bed thinking about critters and friends, he had an idea for a poem give to Dottie. He grabbed some paper and pencil and began to wri

24

I am a boy.
You are a girl.
My hair is short.
You have boing-yoing curls.
I like stripes.
You prefer dots.
But some things we both like A LOT.

Critters that creep
And critters that fly,
Critters that hop
And critters that sigh,
Critters who wiggle and snuggle and purr,
Critters with feathers or covered with fur.

Critters are different
Just like you and me,
But we are all special
In God's family.

I may not look at all like you,
But in ways we're the same, too.
We both love God's critters.
We both like to play.
We both want to be friends
'Cause God made us that way.

Gabe folded up the paper, turned out the light, and put his head on the pillow. Just before going to sleep he whispered, "Thank You, God, for making critter crazy kids like me and Dottie and Josh. In Jesus' name, Amen."

Gabe's Fun Ladybug Facts

1. What's another name for a ladybug?
Ladybird Beetle

2. Can you tell how old a ladybug is by counting its spots?
No, but the number of spots tells us what kind of ladybug it is.

3. How many kinds of ladybugs are there?
There are 5,000 different kinds of ladybugs! Can you believe that? God must have had fun making ladybugs.

4. What do ladybugs eat?
They eat thousands of aphids, which are little white bugs that chew up garden plants. Ladybugs are a gardener's friends.

5. In Russia, they call ladybugs "Bojia karovka" and in French they are called "vache a Dieu." What do you think those names mean in English?
God's little cow.

**6. In 1889, bugs began to kill thousands and thousands of orange, grapefruit, and lemon trees. No one knew what to do

about it. Can you guess what happened to save the trees?

If you guessed "ladybugs to the rescue," you were right! A man named Albert Koebele brought 500 ladybugs to California from Australia and let them go in the fruit groves. In two years, the bad bugs that were eating the fruit were under control. Today in California, ladybugs arc still collected and sold by the thousands to owners of citrus trees.

7. How do ladybugs defend themselves?

They "play possum!" They pull their legs flat against their body and lie very still. They also let a bad-smelling yellowish liquid come out of the joints in their legs when they are handled or touched.

8. What do ladybug babies look like?

The ladybug babies called *larvae* are hatched from eggs. They have long oval bodies that are often longer than the adult ladybugs.

9. After the larvae have eaten about 3,000 aphids, what do they do?

They change into what is called a *pupa* and glue their tummies to the underside of a leaf. If you touch a ladybug pupa, it will make a hammering movement inside.

10. How long does a ladybug stay a pupa?

A ladybug stays a pupa for about seven to ten days, then it pops out to become a ladybug hungry for aphids.

Critter Project

Make a Pet Ladybug Rock

1. Find a light colored, round, smooth rock (any size).

2. Cover a table with newspaper.

3. Use poster paint or markers to paint wings, a head, polka-dots, and six legs on your ladybug. Allow to dry.

4. If you want to make your rock shine, brush it with clear nail polish.

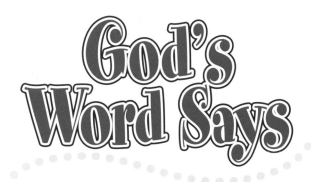

God's Word Says

"I praise you because
You made me in an
amazing and wonderful
way. What you have
done is wonderful. I
know this very well."

Psalm 139:14 (NIV)

The Lovable Ladybug

Age: 4-7 years old

Life Issue: My child needs to understand that God made every person unique and special.

Spiritual Building Block: Accepting Others

Learning Styles

Sight: Using the Internet, an encyclopedia, books, or magazines, look up pictures of people from different countries. Talk to your child about how we differ from people in other countries. How are we the same? Then ask, "How are we different from others in our city, or even our neighborhood? How are we the same?" Pray, thanking God for our individuality..

Sound: Sing the chorus "Jesus Loves the Little Children of the World." Talk to your child about how God created each child special and unique, with individual talents and gifts. Using the illustration of your child's friend, discuss how he or she is different from your child, and then how they are the same. Reinforce how much Jesus loves them both.

Touch: Take modeling clay and spend some time creating critters with your child. Talk about how much fun God must have had creating animals and people. Discuss how we are different from the animals and how we are different from each other. Close by thanking God for our uniqueness.